by Alex Latimer

PICTURE CORGI

for Lily

Penguin's Hidden Talent

A   PICTURE   CORGI   BOOK

978 0 552 562 676   First published in
Great Britain by Picture Corgi, an imprint
of Random House Children's Books   A Random House
Group Company   This edition published 2012

1   3   5   7   9   10   8   6   4   2

Copyright © Alex Latimer, 2012   The right of Alex Latimer to
be identified as the author and illustrator of this work has been
asserted   in accordance with the Copyright, Designs and
Patents Act 1988.   All rights reserved. No part of
this   publication   may   be   reproduced,   stored   in   a
retrieval system, or transmitted in any form or by any
means, electronic, mechanical, photocopying, recording   or
otherwise, without the prior permission of the publishers.
Picture Corgi Books are published by Random House
Children's Books, 61–63 Uxbridge Road, London W5 5SA
www.kidsatrandomhouse.co.uk
www.randomhouse.co.uk
Addresses   for   companies   within
The Random House Group Limited
can   be   found   at:
www.randomhouse.
co.uk/offices.htm
THE RANDOM HOUSE GROUP
Limited Reg. No. 954009
A CIP catalogue record for
this book is available
from the British Library.
Printed and bound
in China.

The BIG annual Talent Show was
just round the corner. . .

...and everyone
was practising.

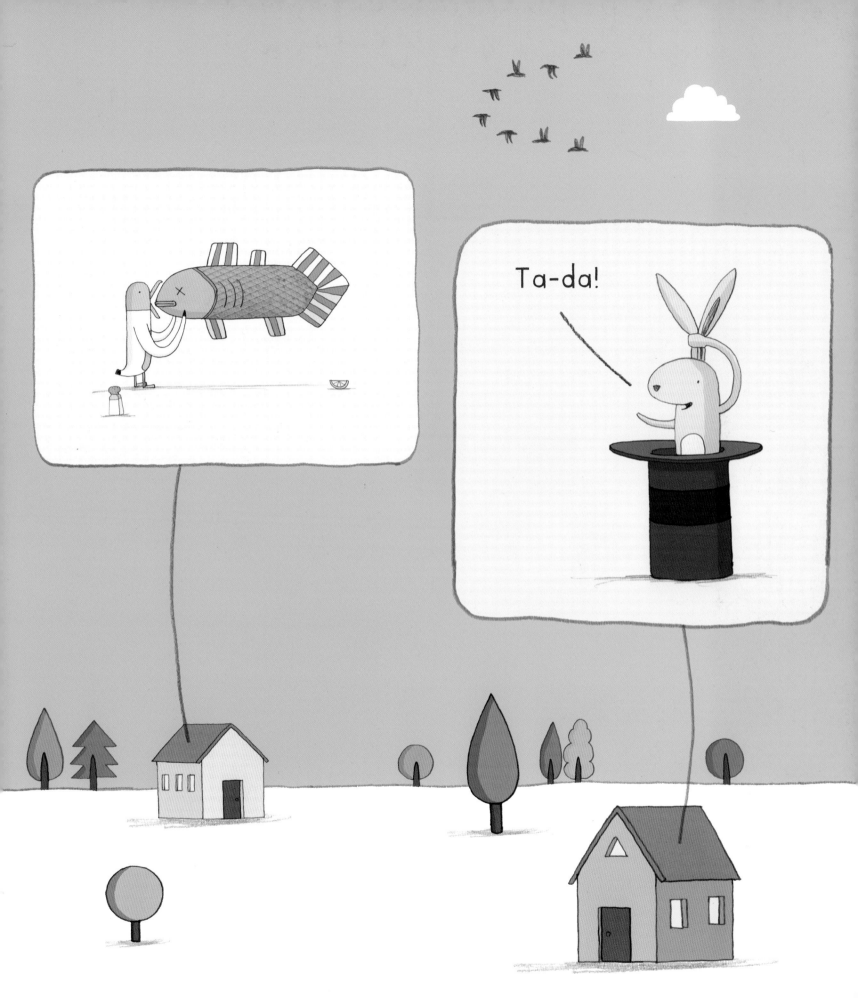

Everyone except Penguin.
Penguin couldn't think what his talent was.

It wasn't baking.

It wasn't map reading.

And it wasn't knitting.

Albatross wanted to help Penguin find his talent.
"Have you ever tried swallowing a whole marlin?" he asked.

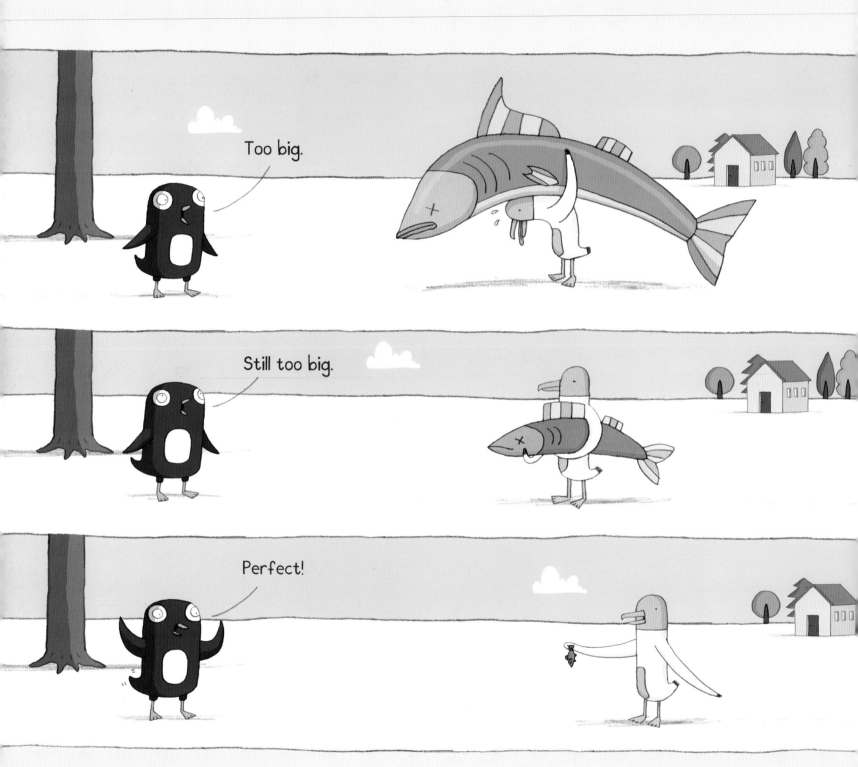

But Penguin could only swallow a sardine.

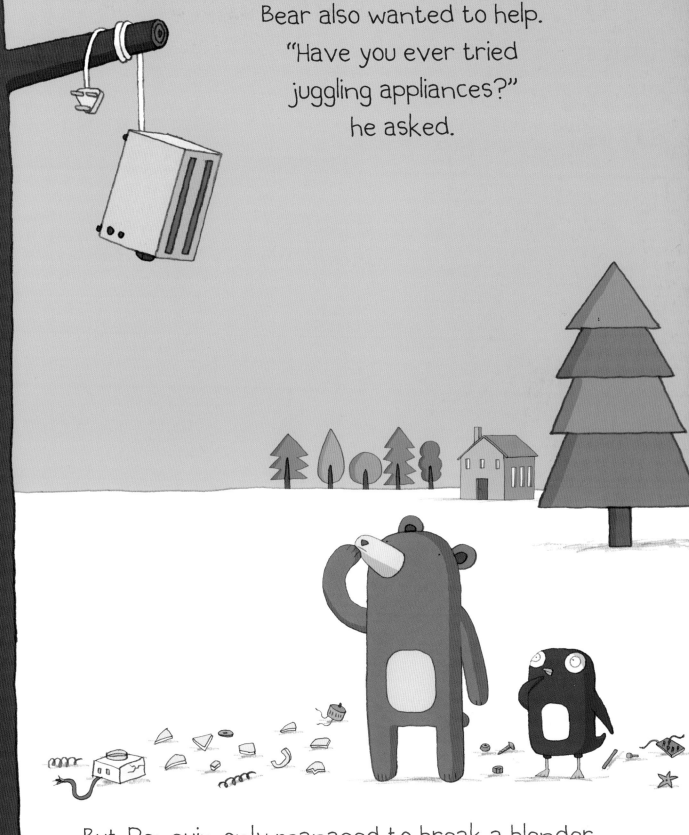

Bear also wanted to help.
"Have you ever tried
juggling appliances?"
he asked.

But Penguin only managed to break a blender
and get a toaster stuck up a tree.

"Have you tried doing magic tricks?" asked Rabbit.
But though Penguin made Rabbit's watch disappear. . .

he couldn't bring it back again.

"Have you tried burping the alphabet?" asked Fox.

But all Penguin could
do was hiccup.

"Don't worry about me," said Penguin. "I'll just help organise the Talent Show. That way I can still be involved, even though I don't have a talent."

So while his friends practised
Penguin drew posters,

made phone calls,

sent emails,

and polished the trophy.

Finally the big day arrived.

The opening ceremony was terrific.

TALENT SHOW

Welcome!

There were fireworks, and jets,
and loads of good music.

Then a guest speaker spoke.

And a famous band played.

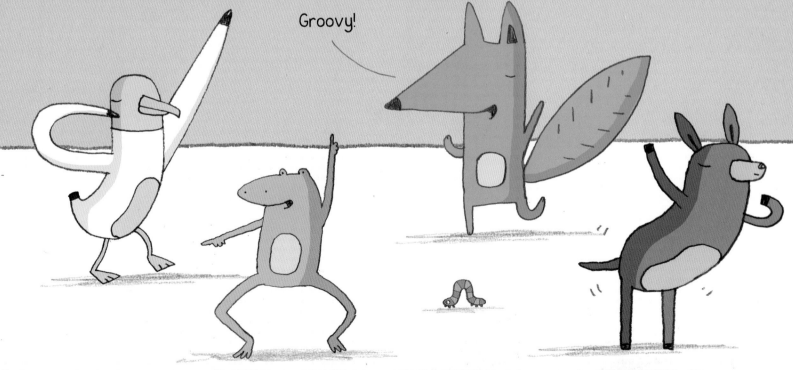

Then the show started.
Albatross, Fox, Bear and Rabbit all did exceptionally well.

$8 \times 8 = 64$

kazam

JUDGES

The judges took ages to count up the points,
but eventually they came to a decision.

"The winner of this year's Talent Show is...

BEAR!

With medals of excellence going to
Albatross, Fox and Rabbit!"

Everyone celebrated.

But not Penguin.

After all, he didn't have a medal.

And he walked slowly home through the snow.

Bear, Albatross, Fox and Rabbit were very worried
about Penguin. They tried to think of a way
to cheer him up.

"I know," said Rabbit.
"Let's throw Penguin a party
to thank him for organising
the Talent Show!"

Everyone agreed that
it was a very good idea.

And they all
worked late
into the night
to organise a
great party.

The next morning, when Penguin came
outside for the newspaper, he found that
his friends had thrown him a party.
And it wasn't a very good one.

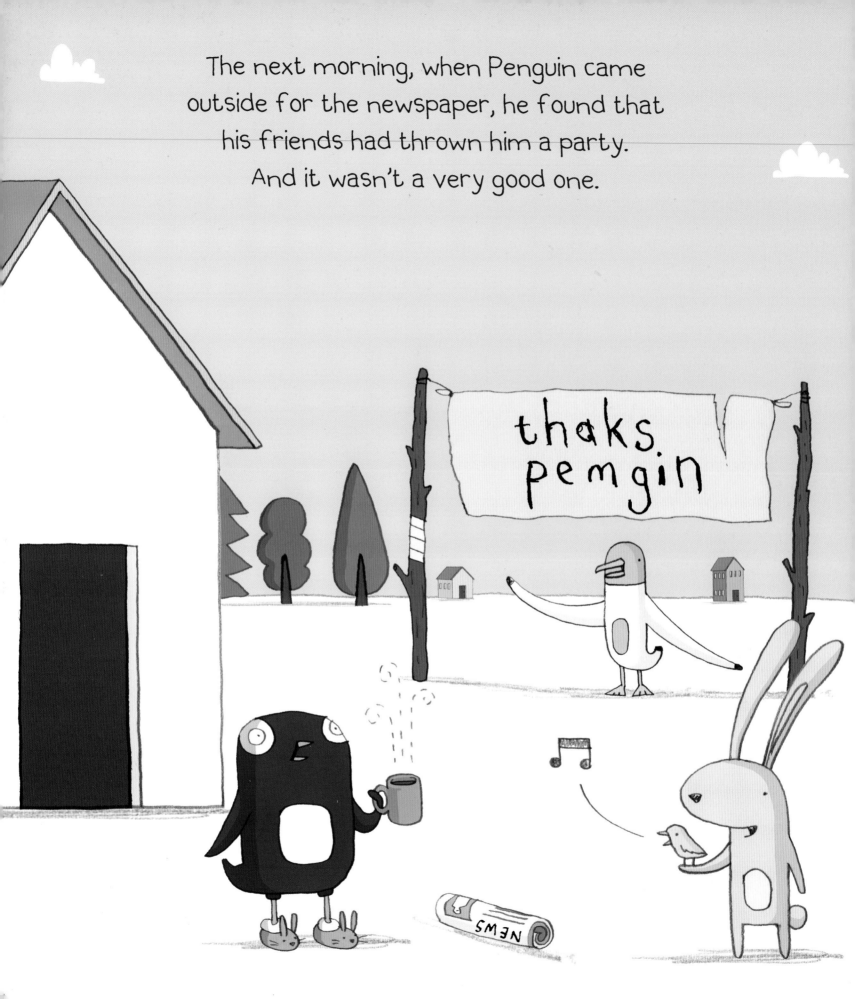

Albatross had made a tatty banner
that said, THAKS PEMGIN.
The only music that Rabbit could organise
was a singing canary.
Fox brought his gran as the guest speaker.
And Bear brought an old loaf of bread
instead of a cake.

And I'll tell you
another thing about
sandwiches...

"If only you'd organised this party, Penguin,"
said Rabbit. "Then it wouldn't be so terrible."

And just
then, Penguin
realised how
talented he
really was.

I don't need a medal.
I need a telephone.

ice cream

What a great
party!

Penguin Rocks

What a great talent!